NORMAN BRIDWELL

Clifford's
BIG BOOK
OF STORIES

Clifford the Big Red Dog

Clifford's Puppy Days

Clifford's Good Deeds

Clifford Gets a Job

Cartwheel B·O·O·K·S ™

SCHOLASTIC INC.

New York   Toronto   London   Auckland   Sydney

To Isabella Carter

Library of Congress Cataloging-in-Publication Data.

Bridwell, Norman.
  Clifford's big book of stories / Norman Bridwell.
    p.   cm.
    Contents: Clifford the big red dog — Clifford's puppy days —
Clifford's good deeds — Clifford gets a job.
                      ISBN 0-590-47925-3
    1. Children's stories, American. [1. Dogs—Fiction.] I. Title.
  PZ7.B7633Clvf 1994   93-31367
  [E]—dc20   CIP
                                                           AC

12 11 10   01 02 03

              Printed in Mexico   49
          First Scholastic printing, March 1994

About Norman Bridwell

When Norman Bridwell was a boy in Kokomo, Indiana, he, like many children, dreamed of owning a dog as big as a horse . . . a dog that he could ride around the neighborhood. He also spent many hours sketching and hoping that one day he would earn his living as an artist.

After attending the John Herron Art Institute in Indianapolis and studying for two years at The Cooper Union in New York City, Bridwell spent 12 years working as a fabric designer and free-lance artist for cartoon strips. One year he fell on particularly difficult times. So, armed with a portfolio of sample drawings, he met with various publishers in an attempt to illustrate children's books.

Says Bridwell, "One editor told me, 'I don't think you can sell this. If you want to illustrate a book, you're going to have to write it, too.'" That's exactly what he did. And Clifford the Big Red Dog was born.

Thirty years later, Clifford is more successful than ever. Bridwell has written more than 30 Clifford books with over 32 million copies in print, placing the clumsy but always lovable canine in all kinds of adventures. In 1990, Clifford made his debut as a balloon in the Macy's Thanksgiving Day Parade.

In 1991, Norman Bridwell was honored with the 14th Annual Jeremiah Ludington Award, given to individuals who have made significant contributions to the world of educational paperbacks.

Bridwell and his family now live in Martha's Vineyard, Massachusetts, in a house with bright-red shutters. One of his two red cars bears the license plate "CLFORD." His wife, Norma, is also an artist and frequently exhibits her watercolors, oils, and prints. The Bridwells have two grown children.

Clifford
THE BIG RED DOG

I'm Emily Elizabeth,
and I have a dog.

My dog is a big red dog.
Other kids I know have dogs, too.
Some are big dogs.

And some are red dogs.
But I have the biggest,
reddest dog on our street.

This is my dog — Clifford.
We have fun together. We play games.

I throw a stick, and he
brings it back to me.

He makes mistakes sometimes.

We play hide-and-seek.
I'm a good hide-and-seek player.

I can find Clifford,
no matter where
he hides.

We play camping out, and I don't need a tent.

He can do tricks, too. He can sit up and beg.

Oh, I know he's not perfect.
He has *some* bad habits.

He runs after cars.
He catches some of them.

He runs after cats, too.
We don't go to the zoo anymore.

He digs up flowers.

Clifford loves to chew shoes.

It's not easy to keep Clifford. He eats and drinks a lot.

His house was a problem, too.

But he's a very good watch dog.

The bad boys don't come around anymore.

One day I gave Clifford a bath.

And I combed his hair,
and took him to a dog show.

I'd like to say Clifford won
first prize. But he didn't.

I don't care.

You can keep all your small dogs. You can keep
all your black, white, brown, and spotted dogs.

I'll keep Clifford. . . . Wouldn't you?

Clifford's
PUPPY DAYS

Hi! We are Clifford and Emily Elizabeth.

Clifford is my dog. He's pretty big.

Clifford wasn't always so big.
When he was a puppy,
he was very, very small.

I had to be careful when I played with him.

He was too small to fetch a ball.

Poor little Clifford.
He wanted to play with my toys.

They were too big.

But he liked the merry-go-round I made for him.

On cold winter days,
Clifford found snuggly
warm places to sleep...

...like my cap.

We put a clock by his bed at night.
The ticking seemed to lull him to sleep.

Once I forgot to turn off the alarm.

At first I gave Clifford baths in our bathtub.

He slipped off the soap one day, and I almost lost him!

After that, I bathed him
in a soup bowl.

Daddy was surprised when
I told him what I had used
for Clifford's bathtub.

It was fun having
such a small puppy.
But Clifford was easy
to lose. One day my
aunt came to visit.

When she left, we
looked all over for
our small red puppy.

My aunt found him in the bake shop.

Clifford was scared.
He plopped into the cream puffs.

Then he ran through the pies.

The baker tried to catch him,
but Clifford climbed up the wedding cake...

...and landed in the whipped cream.

The baker was a little upset.

What a mess! My aunt didn't know what to do.
She didn't want to bring Clifford home looking like that.

29

A small boy with a big dog had an idea.
He said his dog loved whipped cream.

In no time, Clifford was all cleaned up.
I was so happy to have Clifford home
again. The dog who brought him to me
was the biggest dog I had ever seen...

. . .until Clifford grew up.

Clifford's
GOOD DEEDS

Hello, I'm Emily Elizabeth. This is my dog, Clifford.

A boy named Tim lives across the street.

One day Tim said, "I try to do
a good deed every day. If I had Clifford
I could help a lot of people."
I said, "Let's do some good deeds together."

A man was raking leaves. Tim gave him a hand.
Then we helped him put the leaves in his truck.

I didn't know that dry leaves...

...make Clifford sneeze.

The man said he didn't
need any more help.
We went down the street.

We saw a lady painting her fence.
We helped her paint.
When we finished, she thanked us.

Clifford felt so happy
that he wagged his tail.
That was a mistake.
White paint splattered
all over her house.

We said we would paint the rest of her house, too.
The lady said, "Never mind."

Then we saw an old lady
trying to get her kitten
down from a tree.
Tim said, "Clifford, get the kitty."
Clifford bent the limb down
so the lady could reach her kitten.

But his paw slipped.

Clifford moves pretty fast for a big dog.

The lady was glad to get her kitten back.

It didn't take us long to find our next good deed to do.

Somebody had let the air out of the tires
of a car. The man asked if we could help him.

Tim took a rubber tube out of the car...

and stuck it on the tire valve. Then
he told Clifford to blow air through the tube.

Clifford blew.
But he blew a little too hard.

The man felt better when we took his car to a garage.

We saw a small paperboy.
He was so small he couldn't
throw the newspapers
to the doorsteps.

Clifford gave him a hand. I mean a paw.

Clifford was a little too strong.

Nothing seemed to go right for us.
All our good deeds were turning
out wrong.

Then we saw a terrible thing. A man was hurt and lying in the street. Nobody was helping him.

Tim said, "You should never move an injured person." Clifford didn't hear him. He picked the man up.

We started to find a doctor. Oh, dear.

MEN AT WORK

We helped the men get their cable back down the manhole. Tim said, "Clifford, maybe you shouldn't help me anymore."

Clifford felt very sad. He had tried so hard
to do the right things. We headed for home.
Suddenly we heard someone shouting,
"Help! Fire!"

The house on the corner was on fire.
Tim ran to the alarm box
to call the fire department.

Clifford ran to the burning house.
There were two little kids upstairs.
With Clifford's help we got them out safely.

Luckily, there was a swimming pool in the yard.

Clifford put out the fire
just as the firemen were arriving.

The firemen finished the job and thanked us for our help.

That afternoon the mayor gave us each
a medal for our good deeds.

Of course, Clifford got the biggest medal of all.

Clifford
GETS A JOB

Hello —
I'm Emily Elizabeth.

If you don't live on my street, you may not know me . . .

. . . or my dog Clifford.

He's a lot of fun to play with.

There is only one bad thing about Clifford.

He eats a lot of dog food.
And a lot of dog food
costs a lot of money.

We were spending all our money for dog food.
Mother and Daddy didn't know what to do.
"We will have to send Clifford away," they said.

Clifford didn't want to go away.
He made up his mind to get a job
and pay for his own dog food.

He decided to join the circus.
Good Old Clifford.

The circus man liked Clifford. Clifford got the job.

But they put him in the sideshow.
He just sat there.
And people just looked at him.
Clifford wanted to do something.

He peeked into a tent.
He saw little dogs doing tricks.
Clifford wanted to do tricks, too.

So he ran into the tent and he tried
to jump through the hoop —
just like the little dogs.

It didn't work.

In the next ring Clifford saw
a little dog riding on a pony.

Clifford thinks he
can do anything
a little dog can do.

But he can't.

The circus man was angry.
He asked Clifford to leave.
"Don't worry," I said.
"You can get another job."

So we went to see a farmer.

The farmer thought Clifford would be a good farm dog. He said Clifford could work for him.

First Clifford rounded up the cows.

Then Clifford brought home a wagon full of hay. He was doing so well...

. . .and then he saw a rat running to the barn. Clifford knew that rats on a farm are very bad!

So Clifford chased the rat.

Clifford and I started home.
We felt very bad.
Everything had gone wrong.

Suddenly a car came speeding past us.

And right behind it came a police car.
They were chasing robbers.

Clifford took a short cut
through the woods...

...and caught the robbers.

I was very proud.

The Chief of Police
offered Clifford a job
as a police dog.
Now Clifford goes to
work every day.
They don't pay him money.
But...

. . .every week they send Clifford a lot of dog food.
So now we can keep him. Isn't that wonderful?
Good Old Clifford.